This book belongs to:

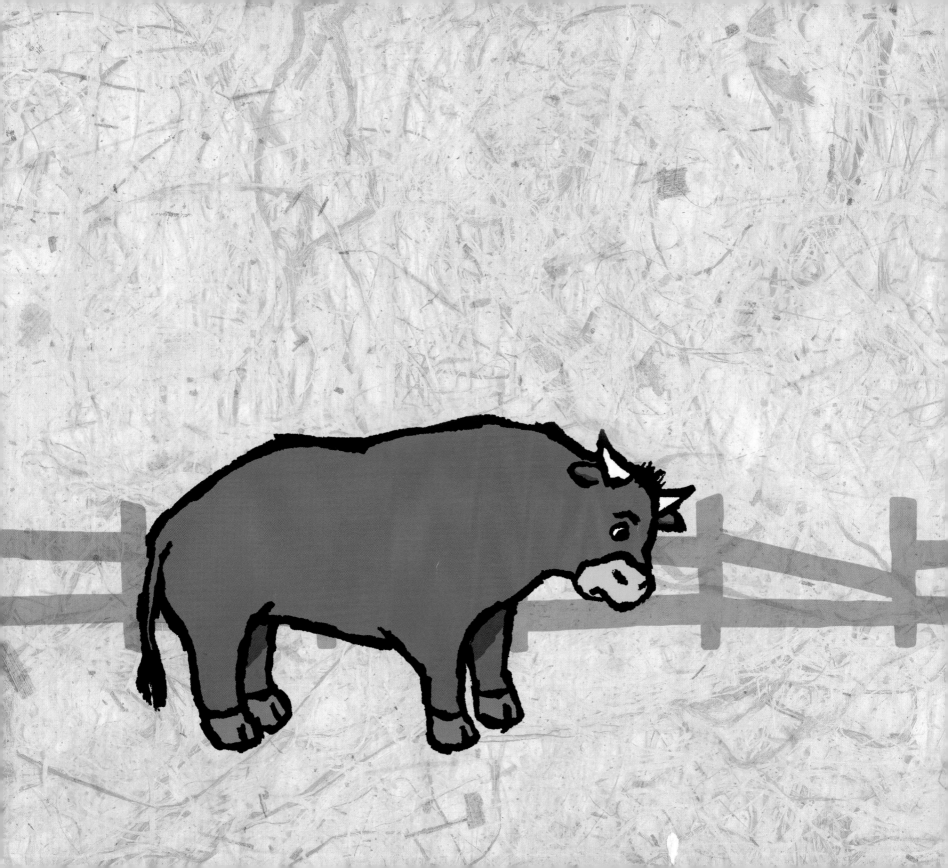

BULLY

LAURA VACCARO SEEGER

ANDERSEN PRESS

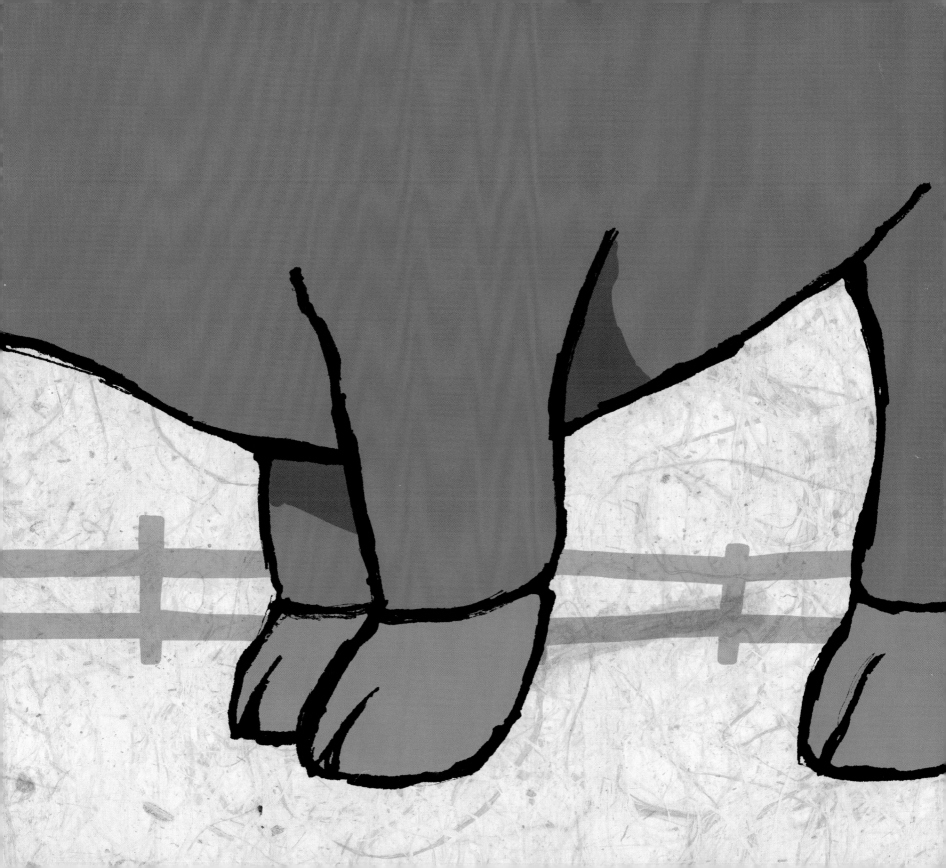

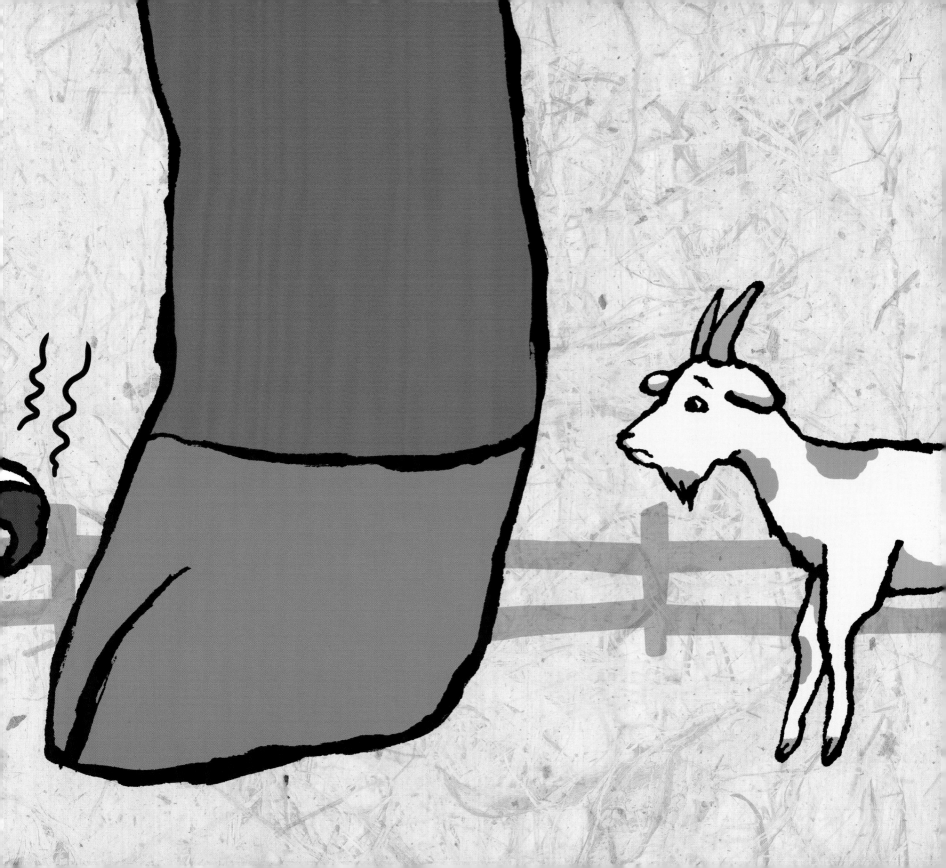

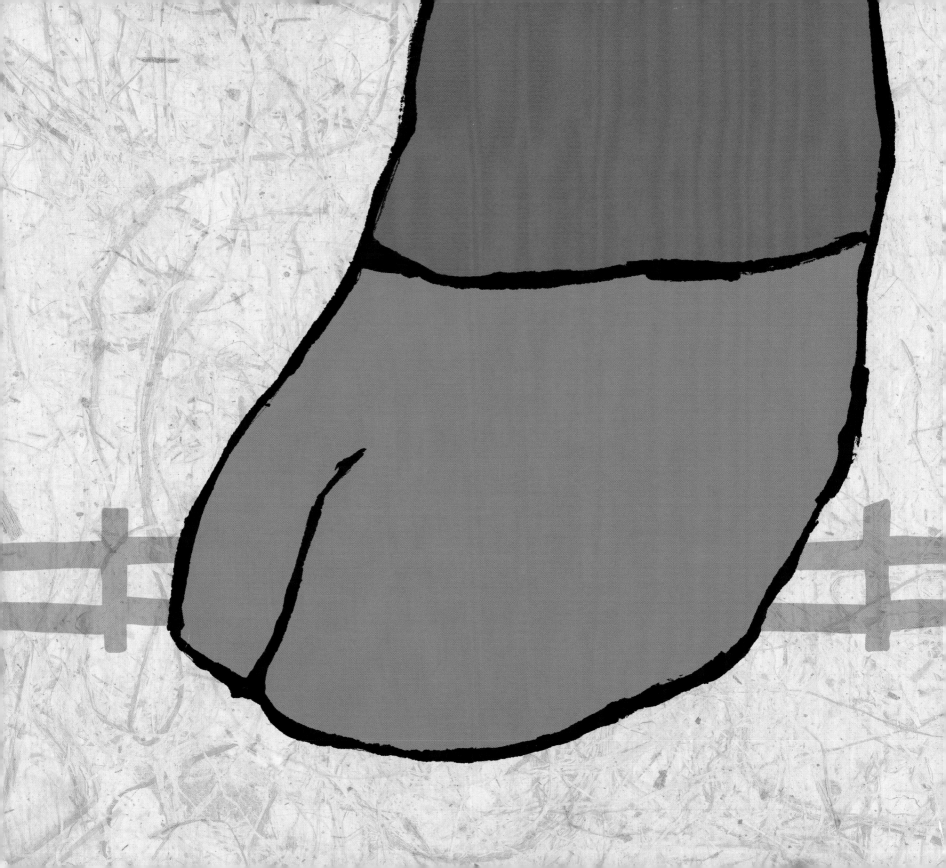

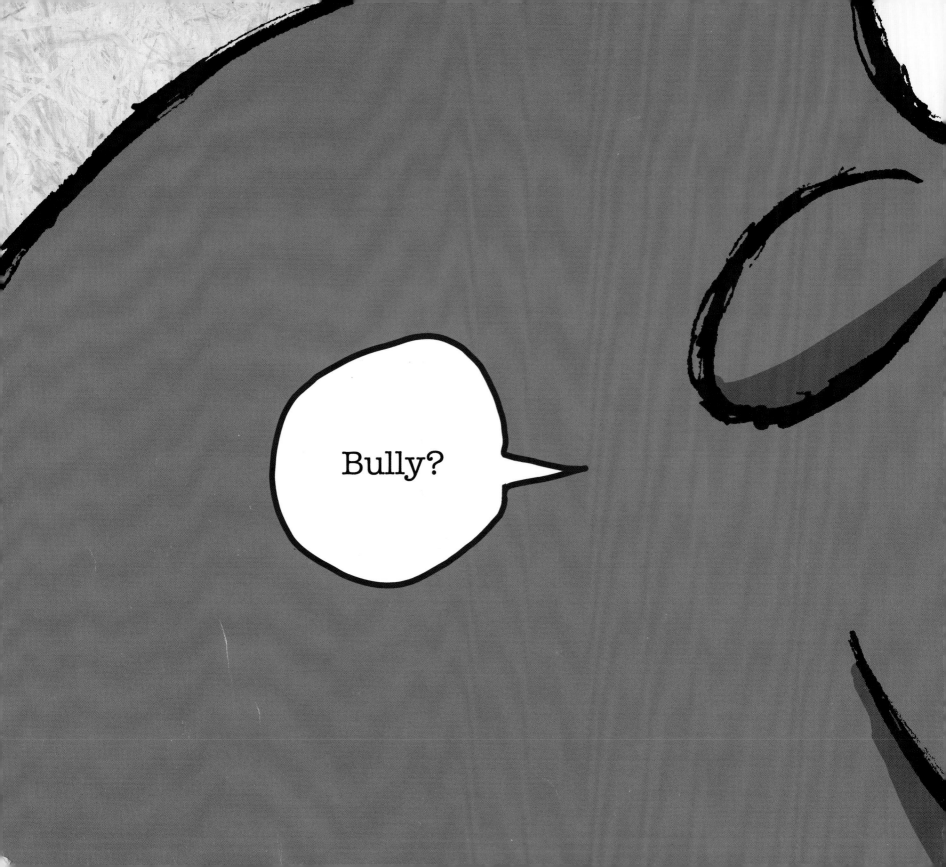

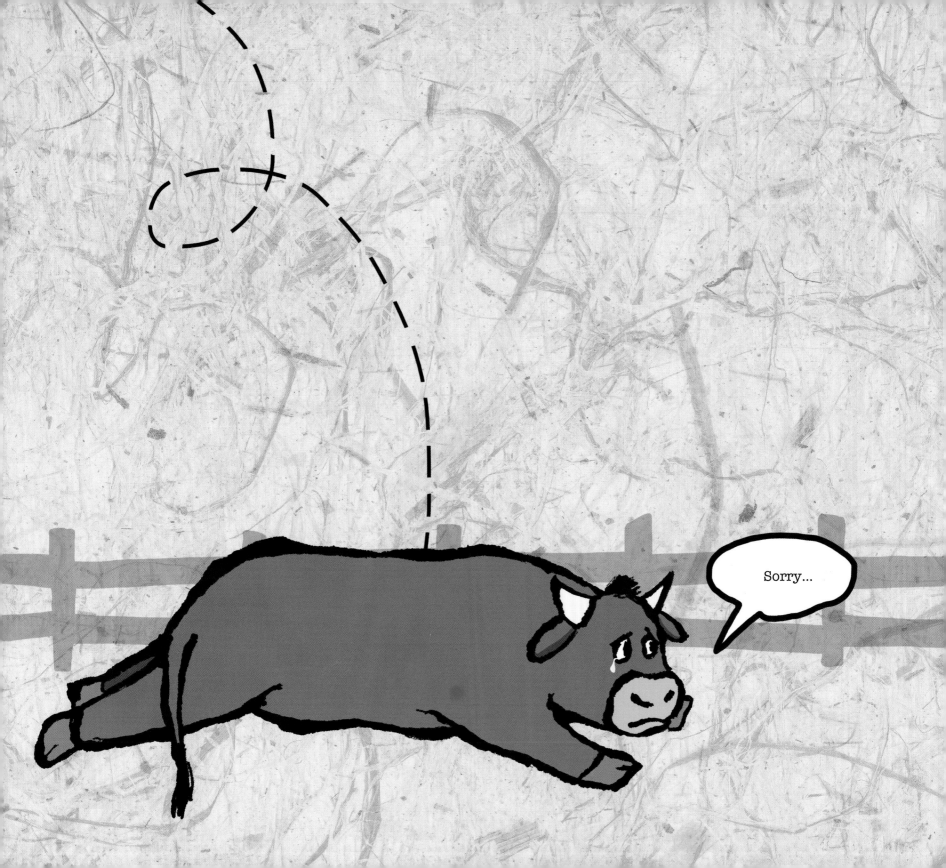

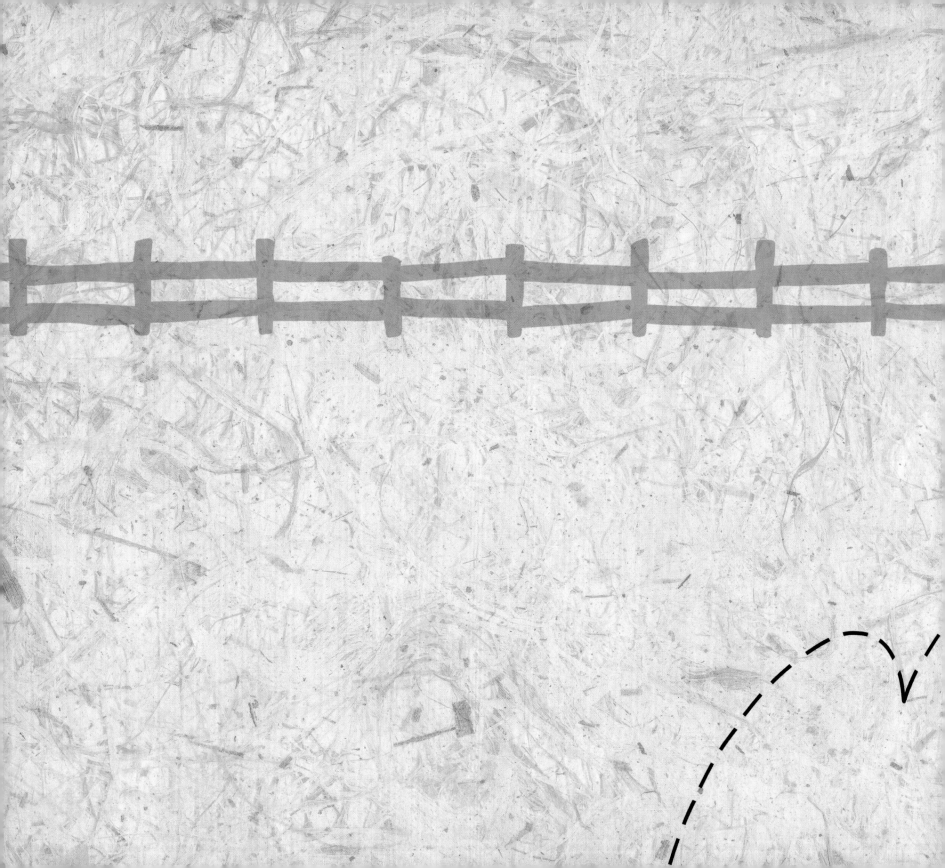

for my niece and nephews,
Laura, Will, Keith, and Philip

First published in Great Britain in 2015 by
Andersen Press Ltd., 20 Vauxhall Bridge Road, London SW1V 2SA.
Published in Australia by
Random House Australia Pty., Level 3, 100 Pacific Highway, North Sydney, NSW 2060.
Published by arrangement with Roaring Brook Press,
a division of Holtzbrinck Publishing Holdings Limited Partnership.
Copyright © Laura Vaccaro Seeger, 2013.
The rights of Laura Vaccaro Seeger to be identified as the author and illustrator
of this work have been asserted by her in accordance with the Copyright,
Designs and Patents Act, 1988.

10 8 6 4 2 1 3 5 7 9

British Library Cataloguing in Publication Data available.

ISBN 978 1 78344 213 3